An I Can Read
Picture Book™

Go Away, Dog

STORY BY JOAN L. NODSET
PICTURES BY PAUL MEISEL

BARNES & NOBLE
NEW YORK

Barnes & Noble Publishing, Inc.
122 Fifth Avenue
New York, NY 10011

ISBN 0-7607-7869-8
Manufactured in China.
07 08 09 MCH 10 9 8 7 6 5 4 3 2

For Aslang Nodset
—J.L.N.

For Steven, Susan, and Jasper
—P.M.

Go away, you bad old dog.
Go away from me.

I don't like you, dog.
I don't like dogs at all.

Big dogs, little dogs.

Any dogs at all.

I don't want that stick.
Don't give it to me.

If I throw the stick,
will you go away?

10

There now, go away
with your stick.

What do you want now?
If I throw it again,
will you go away?

12

Don't jump on me, dog.
I don't like that.

Go away, you old dog.
Go on home now.

14

Don't you have a home?

Well, that is too bad.

But you cannot
come home with me.

16

Don't wag your tail at me.

I don't like dogs.

You are not bad for a dog.

But I don't like dogs.

Say, do that again.

Roll over again, dog.

Say, that is not bad.

Can you shake hands?

This is how

to shake hands.

Don't lick my hand.
Stop that, you old dog.

If I play with you,
will you go away?

All right, let's run, dog.

Can you run
as fast as I can?

You can run fast all right.

That was fun, dog.

Maybe we can play again.

But I have to go home now.

No, you cannot come.
Go away now, dog.

Don't look so sad, dog.

Don't lick my hand.
Can I help it
if you don't have a home?

Why don't you go away?
You like me, don't you,
you old dog?

Well, I like you, too.

All right, I give up.

31

Come on home, dog.

Come on, let's run.